This book belongs to:

....

....

For Nabila - A. H. Benjamin

For F.E.M and H.E.M - Gill McLean

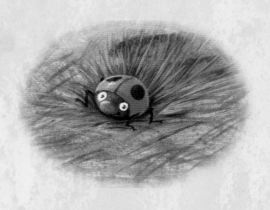

A NEW BURLINGTON BOOK
The Old Brewery
6 Blundell Street
London N7 9BH

Editor: Alexandra Koken
Designer: Verity Clark
Managing Editor: Victoria Garrard
Design Manager: Anna Lubecka

First published in the United States by
QEB Publishing, Inc., 3 Wrigley, Suite A, Irvine, CA 92618

www. qed-publishing.co.uk

A CIP record for this book is available from the Library of Congress.

ISBN 978 1 78171 377 8

Printed in China

The Nearsighted Giraffe

A. H. Benjamin · Gill McLean

NEW
BURLINGTON
BOOKS

Giraffe couldn't see
very well.

She tripped over Snake
and got in a huge tangle.

"You need glasses!" the other animals cried.

So they made her a pair.

"I'm not wearing them," said Giraffe. "A giraffe in glasses would look silly!"

And she walked off.

Giraffe would not wear the glasses—
even after she banged her
head on a branch.

"I'll wear a bicycle
helmet," she said,
"to protect my head."

So from then on, Giraffe wore a bicycle helmet.

"What's she doing?"
the animals asked each other.

Giraffe would not
wear the glasses—

even after she

crashed

into Rhino.

"I'll wear a bell on my tail," she said.
"Then everyone will hear me coming."

So Giraffe wore a bicycle helmet and a bell.

"How silly!"
Lion grumbled.

Giraffe would not wear
the glasses—even after
she hurt her foot on
a rock.

"I'll wear boots," she said.
"That way my feet will
be safe."

So Giraffe wore a bicycle
helmet, a bell, and boots.

"She's getting worse,"
Elephant whispered.

Giraffe would not wear the glasses—even after she sat on a thorny bush.

"I'll wear a pillow," she said. "It will protect my bottom."

So Giraffe wore a bicycle helmet,
a bell, boots, and a pillow.

"How odd!"
everyone said.

Giraffe would not wear
the glasses—even after she
fell into the river.

"I'll wear an inflatable ring," she said, "to keep me afloat if I fall in the water."

"She's crazy!" Hippo laughed.

So Giraffe wore a bicycle helmet, a bell, boots, a pillow, and an inflatable ring.

Giraffe would not wear the glasses—even after she tumbled into a hole.

"I'll carry a ladder with me," she said. "Then if I fall in a hole, I'll be able to climb out."

So Giraffe wore a bicycle
helmet, a bell, boots,
a pillow, and an
inflatable ring—

and she carried a ladder
over her back!

"How ridiculous!"
everyone said.

The other animals
felt sorry for Giraffe.

"If only she could
see herself," Cheetah said.

One night Cheetah had an idea. He crept up to Giraffe while she was sleeping and put the glasses on her...

She took off

the bicycle helmet,

the bell,

the boots,

the pillow,

the inflatable ring,

and finally the ladder.

Giraffe looked back in the pool and noticed the glasses perched on her nose.

"Hmmm," she smiled, pleased. "I look really good!"

"Yes, you do!" everyone cheered.

Finally able to see, Giraffe stepped over a ladybug, and happily strolled off.

Next steps

Show the children the cover again. Could they have guessed what the story is about just from looking at the cover?

Do the children know the term nearsighted? Explain it to them. Do the children wear glasses, or know any children that do? How do they feel about glasses? Did they feel shy or concerned when they started wearing them, or did they feel good in them? Discuss other special devices such as a retainer, crutches, and hearing aids, and why they are sometimes needed.

Ask the children if they have seen a real giraffe. Perhaps they've seen one in a zoo, or if they're lucky in the wild. Explain to the children that giraffes live in Africa, where many different animals live. Can the children name any?

In the story, Giraffe wouldn't wear the glasses her friends made for her. Even when bad things started happening to her she found excuses not to wear them. Can the children think of other excuses Giraffe might make? What excuses would they make if they didn't want to do something?

Ask the children to draw pictures of different animals wearing glasses. Discuss how the animals look. Do they look stylish, clever, pretty, or even funny? What kind of glasses would an elephant wear? Or a leopard? Or a lemur?